THIS BOOK BELONGS TO

Icon Publishing Limited
P. O. Box OD 972
Odorkor, Accra
Ghana
www.facebook.com/myicongh
www.twitter.com/myicongh
+233 (0)23 3505 055,

iconpublishingltd@gmail.com
iconpublishing@ymail.com
enquiries.icongh@gmail.com

Cover and Interior Design by iCON-gh +233 24 4890 432

ISBN: 978-9988-8566-2-5

GOD'S CHALLENGE TO WISE PEOPLE

A GHANAIAN FOLKTALE

Dan Odei

Kwame Insaidoo

Long, long ago, God threw a big challenge out to all the wisest people in the world and promised that any person who succeeded in unravelling the challenge would be declared the wisest person in the whole world. The challenge, for any person who dared, was to take only one cob of corn and use it to capture an entire city.

Many people wondered how on earth one could use one corncob to capture an entire city, but that was the challenge God was throwing out to only the wisest people on earth. Many people who heard of this challenge simply threw their hands up, claiming that it would be impossible to fulfill such an outrageous challenge, but when Ananse heard about it, he vowed that he would be able to accomplish what God had asked in less than a week.

Many people scoffed at Ananse's boastfulness and arrogance, while some even laughed and said, "The super intelligent and wise people could not meet God's challenge, so who is this Ananse — with his average wisdom and intelligence—to waste God's and everybody's time with his forward, know-it-all attitude?"

But despite the negative protestations of all the naysayer, Ananse ventured to capture a big city with only a cob of corn.

Many people wondered how Ananse could do such a thing since there was plenty of food all over the villages, towns, and cities and many people ate their fill and even threw away their leftovers. So, who in their right mind would give away a whole city for just one measly corncob? Others said, "Well, knowing Ananse and his trickery, let's wait and see where the wind will blow. Perhaps a good wind will come and bring him the good fortune he needs to win God's award, but he'll need all the luck he can get to succeed."

Early the next morning Ananse bade the villagers farewell as he embarked on his mission to accomplish the impossible task of using a corn of cob to capture an entire city. He took one corncob and an empty sack, and even the empty sack was thoroughly inspected by the security agents as Ananse left the village to ensure that it was indeed empty.

*Ananse embarking on his mission to accomplish the
impossible task*

Ananse went first to a small town where an old farmer had a large poultry farm. Ananse beamed a cheerful smile when he met the old farmer and informed him that he had an urgent message that could not wait. He insisted on having a private conversation with the man. The old farmer, wondering what urgent message a stranger could have for him, asked Ananse to come inside his house so he could deliver the message. Ananse deliberately left the cob of corn outside on the poultry farm, where hundreds of live chickens and hens were running wild, and entered into the old farmer's house.

In the house, Ananse engaged the farmer in several discussions about the benefits of the poultry farm in the community and how he wished his community had such well-kept and well-run farms. Ananse praised the old farmer for the good work he was doing in the community and asked the man to show him how he could begin to raise chickens success-fully. Ananse spent over three hours in the old man's house before taking his leave.

When Ananse returned to his sack, he saw that his farmer's chickens had devoured his corn, and he angrily complained, "What happened here? I thought you were a good friend, but see what your chickens and hens have done to the corn God gave me to preserve for a special day? You know, God intended for this special corn to be used to save the lives of many hungry people because it grows quickly and it's easily harvested in less than two months. Hunger as we know it would have been banished from the earth. But now that your chickens have devoured it, I am in a big trouble with God. Please help me. Give me ideas about what to tell God about his special corn."

Ananse went on to tell the old farmer that he could spare them all the troubles and aggravations and questions from God if he could give Ananse only one chicken to prove to God that all he had done was just exchange a corncob for one chicken. Ananse assured the old man that he would spare himself any trouble from God if he received just one chicken from his poultry farm.

The old farmer calculated his risks and replied, "You know, my friend, I lived peacefully here on my farm with no troubles until now, and I am very sorry that my chickens devoured the special corn God gave you. If it will please God, please take one—indeed take any one of the chickens from my farm, if it will take your troubles away."

Ananse quickly grabbed one of the biggest hens on the farm and bade the farmer good-bye, smiling all the way out of the farm.

Ananse walked many miles until he reached a peace-loving shepherd who had a large flock of sheep that was grazing on beautiful. rolling grassland. When Ananse saw the healthy-looking flock of sheep running wild on the grassland, he smiled to himself and muttered, "I am on my way to winning God's challenge with all these beauties roaming around here. Let me slowly take my time to approach the owner of this flock of sheep. Ananse left his large hen at the centre of the meadow, with all the sheep roaming around the hen, and went quickly to the shepherd and began entangling him with unnecessary conversation.

"Hey, young man," he said, "help me with a riddle my father wants me to solve. The riddle goes like this: Who would you save first if you were in a large ocean with your father, wife, and mother, and the boat capsized?" The man replied that he would save his wife first because she was the mother of his children and he would need her to help nurture them. "I must be in love with her, so I have an obligation to save her first," he added.

Ananse told the shepherd that he was a fool because, although he had only one mother but could get as many wives as he wanted. Ananse explained that he should go ahead and save his mother and let his wife drown. "Don't you see how many women divorce their husbands when they get more money than their husbands? And don't you see how many wives disrespect their husbands and secretly fool around with other lovers?"

The shepherd was enjoying the long conversation with Ananse, so they kept talking late into the night and finally went to sleep under a large tree.

The next day Ananse and the shepherd were shocked to see that some of the sheep had killed Ananse's large hen and scattered its feathers all over the meadow. The shepherd apologized profusely to Ananse and said he was very sorry for what his sheep had done to Ananse's hen.

Ananse responded, "You are one of the nicest men I have ever met, and you have taken good care of me ever since I came here, so I sincerely respect you. My only problem that I need your help with is this dead hen.

"You know," he continued, "this hen belongs to Almighty God, and I am deafly afraid of what he will do to me if I do not return the hen to him alive. Please help me ... What can I do to appease him?"

The good shepherd asked Ananse if he could take one of his sheep to replace God's hen. Ananse replied, "Why would you give such a large sheep for one small hen? Oh, you are such a sweet man to even entertain such a thought."

The shepherd, who did not want to have anything to do with Ananse and his trickery, insisted that he should take one of the sheep with him because he did not want to incur God's wrath.

Ananse responded, "Well, if you insist, I have no choice but to show God that a kindhearted shepherd has replaced the hen that was killed by offering up a large sheep, and God should continue to bless you."

Ananse took the biggest of large sheep, as the shepherd instructed, and with a smile moved quickly away from the shepherd and his flock. Within minutes, Ananse, running with the sheep, was far away from the meadow. Ananse was so happy that he began to sing and dance. He sang:

Papa Ananse ee, Papa Ananse ee, Papa Ananse ee
I have come all the way from my village
To enter into an unwinnable contest
I promised myself that I would prevail
And win God's award
No one dared take God up on this unwinnable challenge
I took a corncob and all my peers laughed at my folly
And swore I could prevail in this seemingly unwinnable contest
With the corncob, I got a large hen
And now I have a live sheep
I know I will definitely win God's award
I am on my way to success

Ananse continued to sing and sometimes hum melodious songs, as he continued to be relentlessly optimistic about winning God's challenge of using a single corncob to capture an entire city.

Ananse kept walking through the grasslands and through mountain chains, and finally he came upon a large field with hundreds of roaming cattle. Ananse desperately looked for the owner of the cattle; he searched and searched until he found the owner and then begged him for a place to spend the night, telling him, "I have travelled all night with my beloved sheep through the jungles and across swollen rivers infested with crocodiles, and now we are tired and looking for a place to spend the night. Please help us."

The owner of the cattle was sympathetic to Ananse and his sheep, so he offered Ananse a nice hut to spend the night; but before Ananse went to sleep he deliberately left his sheep in the midst of the wild bulls.

The next morning when Ananse woke up, he was saddened to see that the wild bulls had trampled and killed his beloved sheep. He began to weep loudly and uncontrollably as the young cattle herders began to comfort him, but he could not stop—until the cattle owner asked how he could compensate him.

Ananse explained to the owner, "You see, the sheep that was killed by your wild bulls was a special sheep that belonged to God. I do not want the wrath of God to befall your herd, but if you do not do something about your bulls killing God's sheep, maybe, just maybe—and we never can tell—God's wrath will bring a terrible disease to kill many of your cattle."

The owner of the cattle became fearful at the thought of losing any of his cows, let alone that a disease from God might kill dozens of his well-cultivated cattle, so he offered to give Ananse anything he asked for. Ananse replied that he was grateful to the owner for giving him a place to sleep when he most needed it and did not want to inconvenience him but only wanted him to make some gesture of compensation.

The owner of the herd told Ananse that it was better to lose one cow than to lose a whole herd of cattle, so he asked Ananse to look through the entire herd and select any one of the bulls to take with him and continue with his journey to please God. The owner knew that in a short time his cows could give birth to many more, so giving one cow to Ananse for him to take his trouble away was the smartest thing to do.

Ananse carefully looked through the entire herd and took one big bull with him. Then he bade the owner farewell and left. He proudly moved along with his cow and hummed one melody after another, happily making his way along the dusty road. Eventually, he came across a group of people who were wailing and sobbing and carrying a coffin on their way to bury a dead person. Ananse hurried to the group and offered to take the dead body from them. The family protested, but Ananse insisted that they give the body to him. He offered the cow he had in exchange for the dead body. The family was amazed at the uneven exchange, but who could turn down a large cow or bull for a dead body?

Ananse took the dead body and put it on his shoulder and then left the wailing party behind on his way to win God's award. He carried the dead body on his shoulders until he reached the outskirts of a big city and quickly asked to be taken to the king's palace.

When Ananse arrived at the palace he told the king that he was a special messenger from God, sent to deliver an important message to him. But, he said, he and his friend were so tired they would not be able to deliver their message in its entirety until after they got enough rest. Ananse further suggested that his friend was so dead tired that he could not even raise his head or speak until he got some rest and needed to be put to bed immediately with the servants in the servants' quarters.

The happy-go-lucky king ordered his servants to take Ananse's friend to their quarters, and they obliged,

Ananse carrying the dead body on his shoulders

while Ananse was given a room in the palace. The king anxiously waited to hear the special message from God.

The next day, when everyone woke up, Ananse's friend did not wake up, and Ananse became terribly upset. He complained bitterly to the king that his servants had deliberately and maliciously strangled his friend to death. Furthermore, Ananse frightened the king by reminding him, "You know, king, my friend was an apostle from God who was sent to the city to ward off an impending catastrophic plague approaching the city that could wipe out thousands of citizens, even you and your immediate family." Ananse continued to frighten the king by adding, "The impending disaster would be so catastrophic that after most of the inhabitants are killed by the plague and other disasters, the remaining people will rebel and dethrone you and your elders and kill as many of the elders as they possible can." Ananse told the king that the only possible alternative to the impending catastrophe was for the king to appoint him, Ananse, as the king of the city. "As the new king, I will communicate with God and explain the circumstances of the death of his apostle and remove any curse from the city."

The king was relieved that Ananse could provide him with an alternate means to save his city and family from the impending destruction, and he called a great gathering at the centre of the city and informed them of God's chosen apostle and leader for their city. He said he would resign as their king so that Ananse could become their next king. The elders of the city installed Ananse as their new king, and God declared him not only the wisest man on earth but also the wisest king on earth, because he had done the impossible: capture a city by using only one cob of corn. Ananse sang his melodious song after he was installed as king:

Listen to my song, people
God threw a challenge, many people laughed at me
When I began, but despite their laughter and cynicism
I dogmatically set out with a corncob and got my first hen
From the hen, I got the sheep, and then the cow, and my
"tired" apostle
And eventually I captured a city
Always remember, do not let naysayer discourage you in
your dreams
For if you persist and persevere you'll always attain
success

Moral Lessons

There are quite a few morals to this story. The first lesson for all of us is the fine art of persistence and perseverance; we must not give up on our dreams but must persist in whatever goals we set for ourselves. We should be determined and forceful in attaining our goals and persist through the challenges and vicissitudes that may come our way, never giving up until we succeed. If Ananse had not been so determined, he could not have gone through all the problems and challenges that confronted him; but Ananse persisted and finally succeeded. We do not, however, subscribe to the lies, trickery, immorality, and deceptive methods Ananse employed to succeed; people sometimes do—and should—recoil from a person who employs trickery and devious means to succeed.

Additionally, the story teaches us to be careful of smiling people who use the name of God to deceive other people, like Ananse did. We should all be vigilant to look into the motives of such people before buying their messages from God.

Finally, we all have the responsibility to protect ourselves and our hard-earned property and refuse to let people abuse us or take advantage of us by tricking us to get what belongs to us. You see, Ananse should not have been allowed to leave his corn on the poultry farm where the chickens might get to it. Furthermore, the owners of the sheep and cattle should have been vigilant and protected themselves from ruthless strangers like Ananse who trespassed on their properties only to benefit from their hard work. It was basically through lies, deception, and trickery that Ananse succeeded in duping these honest and hardworking people. These people were too trusting for their own good; such people should in future closely examine the motives of strangers, challenging them and asking plenty of questions and not being easily satisfied with their answers. If possible, they should find out more about the total strangers they meet before getting involved with them.

Answer the following questions:

1. a) What was God's challenge to all wise people in the world?

    b) What was the promised reward?

2. What was the reaction of the people when Ananse vowed that he could accomplish what God had asked in less than a week?

3. Describe in vivid detail from the very first small town Ananse entered how he was able to win God's challenge?

4. How would you describe the king who proclaimed Ananse as God's chosen apostle and leader for their city and subsequently installed him as a successor?

5. What have you learned from this folktale?

6. Find the meaning of the following words in the dictionary and use them in sentences of your own,
    i. Unravelling
    ii. Outrageous
    iii. Scoffed
    iv. Protestations
    v. Naysayer
    vi. Measly
    vii. Devoured

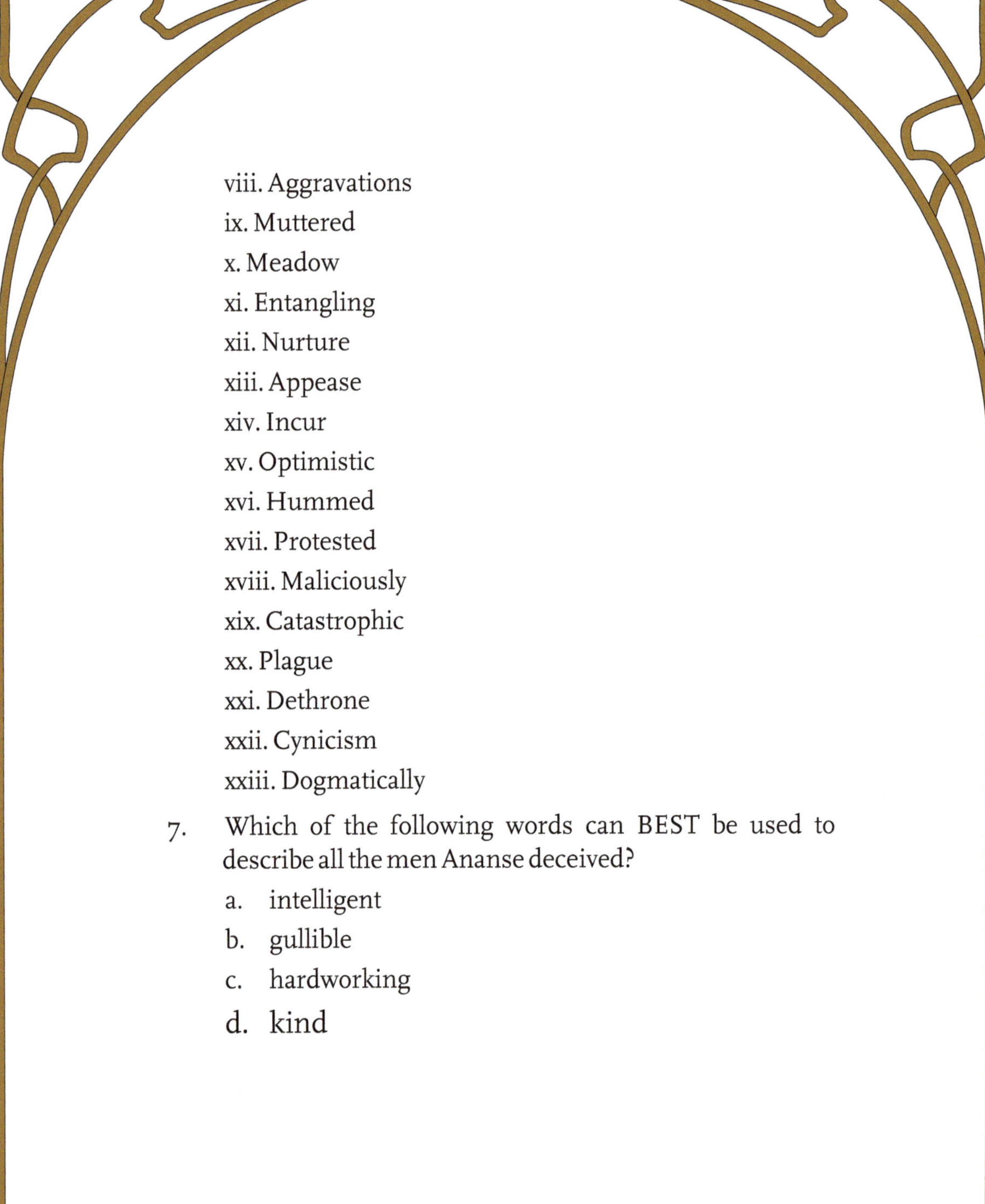

viii. Aggravations

ix. Muttered

x. Meadow

xi. Entangling

xii. Nurture

xiii. Appease

xiv. Incur

xv. Optimistic

xvi. Hummed

xvii. Protested

xviii. Maliciously

xix. Catastrophic

xx. Plague

xxi. Dethrone

xxii. Cynicism

xxiii. Dogmatically

7. Which of the following words can BEST be used to describe all the men Ananse deceived?

a. intelligent

b. gullible

c. hardworking

d. kind

Answer the questions here.

Answer the questions here.